USBORNE HOTSHOTS

LETTERING

USBORNE HOTSHOTS
LETTERING

Edited by Lisa Miles

*Illustrated by Fiona Brown, Guy Smith,
Chris Smedley and Robin Lawrie*

*Hand lettering by David Young
Photographs by Howard Allman*

*Series editor: Judy Tatchell
Series designer: Ruth Russell*

With thanks to Graham Peet

CONTENTS

Lettering techniques

Lettering is all around you, in books, magazines and newspapers, and on food wrappers, shop signs and clothes. The important thing about lettering is that it should always make its message clear.

Style tips

A short message looks exciting and comes across well if you pick a lettering pattern or style that suits the message. The way letters look can say almost as much as the words they form.

Keeping letters even

Keep your letters even by drawing them between faint pencil rules, called guidelines. Unless you want very thin or fat letters, the height of the letter should be between three and nine times the thickest part of the letter.

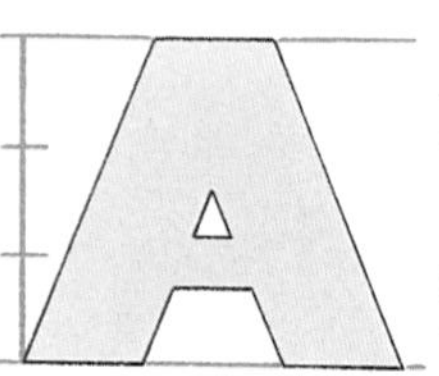

Height of letter is three times the thickest part of the letter.

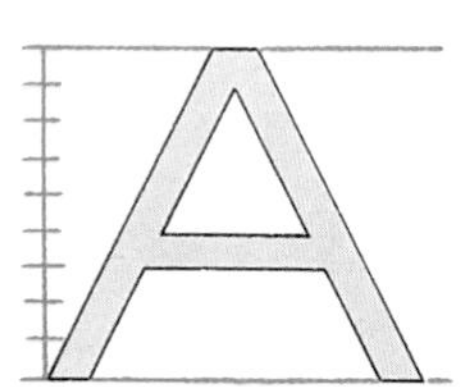

Height of letter is nine times the thickest part of the letter.

Small letters

Small (lower case) letters are just over half as tall as capital (upper case) letters. Letter sticks (ascenders) and tails (descenders) extend above and below guidelines by about the same amount.

baggy pants

Flowing letters

Use an italic nib (see pages 26-27) to do a flowing, joined-up style. Try using just one guideline through the middle of the letters. This keeps them level, but looking less rigid.

Single guideline through middle of letters.

Try curving the guideline for a flowing shape.

Atmospheric lettering

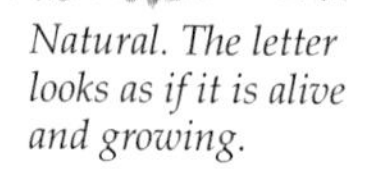

Natural. The letter looks as if it is alive and growing.

Letter can set a scene or create an atmosphere by their shape or the way they are decorated. The letters on this page have had their shapes adapted or decorated for certain effects. Different tones also help to give atmosphere.

Decorating letters is called illumination. You can find out more on pages 18-19.

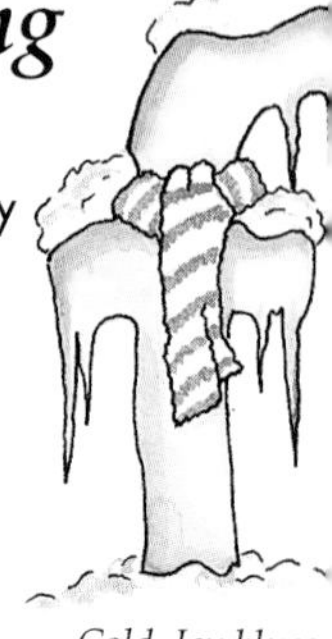

Cold. Icy blues and greens are cold shades.

Marine. The outline ripples, like water.

Ghoulish. Use images commonly found in horror movies and stories.

Hot. Reds, oranges and yellows are warm shades.

Festive. Party equipment provides decoration for this letter.

Secret messages

A quick way to do lettering without doing it by hand is to use newspaper and magazine print. Here, different styles have been torn out roughly. This is supposed to resemble an anonymous message such as a kidnap ransom note.

You could use this sort of style for a joke. No one would expect a Valentine's Day message to be written in such a threatening style.

You can use whole words or make them up out of separate letters. Vary the size and style of the letters.

Ancient letters

These letters look old and battered. You can get this effect by enlarging typed letters lots of times on a photocopier. The letters break up and become more ragged as tiny faults get bigger and bigger.

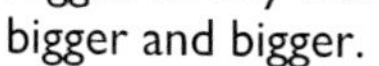

These letters have been photocopied 20 times and enlarged by 100% each time.

Letters typed on a typewriter with a fabric ribbon produce the best results, especially if the ribbon is fairly worn.

"Graffiti" styles

Graffiti styles developed when people began spraying their names on subway trains and walls in New York in the 1960s. It is illegal to write on walls but you can use the style on paper.

Graffiti masterpieces

Elaborate, highly-decorated bits of graffiti are known as "pieces", short for masterpieces. Here are some examples.

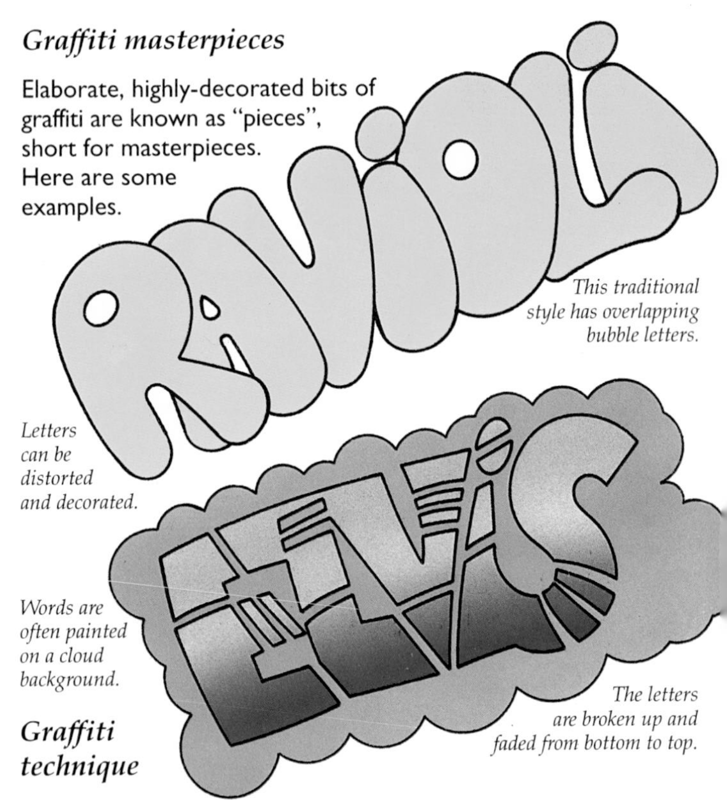

This traditional style has overlapping bubble letters.

Letters can be distorted and decorated.

Words are often painted on a cloud background.

The letters are broken up and faded from bottom to top.

Graffiti technique

Good graffiti needs careful planning. Sketch your idea in rough before doing the real thing.

1. Roughly block out the letters in your piece of graffiti.

2. Add a cloud background, scenery and decoration.

3. Fill in the shapes. Add an outline around the letters.

Inventing a tag

A tag is a graffiti writer's signature – usually a nickname. You could invent a tag and use it instead of signing your real name. Your tag should be striking.

NIGE

A tag needs to be quick to write. The quickest sort is one shade only.

This sort of tag is called a throw-up. It has an outline around a single shade.

Materials

Spray paints cover large areas quickly. One way to copy this effect is to use marker pens. You can buy these from art shops. They are expensive, though, so you could try using ordinary felt tips instead. The wider the tip, the better.

Marker pens

This complex style has a pattern of interlocking letters which can be quite difficult to read. It is called wildstyle.

Time travel

Give your letters a historical feel by copying the different styles people used in the past. Each historical age had its own distinctive style of lettering.

This style, called gothic style, is based on a centuries-old script. It has often been used for horror film and story titles. To write in gothic script, you need a broad italic pen. If you don't have one, try drawing the letter outlines and filling them in. There is a gothic-style alphabet to copy on page 30.

In a creepy castle

The letters are squarish and angular.

Small letters are mostly made up of straight lines.

Capital letters can be decorative.

Art Nouveau

In the late 19th century, an artistic style called Art Nouveau developed. Art Nouveau lettering looks good when it is designed into a picture. The letters below are natural shapes, like the trees.

Letters are part of the picture, rather than on top of it.

1930s style

1930s design was elegant and precise. The shapes needed no decoration. For capital letters, draw a simple letter shape. Then thicken one side with downstrokes. Small letters have a round shape and a uniform thickness.

This style is good for short, stylish messages.

Making posters

You could use tinted paper.

Lettering on a poster should catch people's attention and be easy to read from a distance. The size of the paper you use depends on how far away you want the poster to be seen from. Leaving space around your lettering will help it to stand out.

Designing a poster

First, write down what you want to say. Keep it simple.

Then divide the message up and number the parts in order of importance. You need to make the most important words stand out.

Finally, choose a suitable style for the message and any illustration on the poster.

Drop shadows

To do a drop shadow, draw a letter. Then copy the outline a little to one side and above or below the letter shape. Fill in the shadow a darker shade.

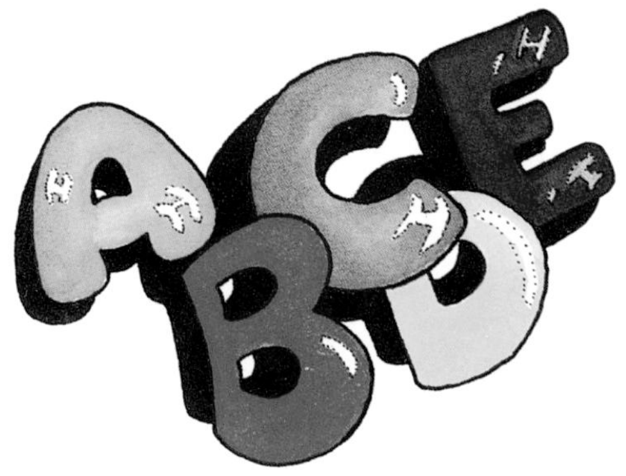

Making letters bigger

You can draw big letters on your poster by enlarging small letters to the size you want, using a grid. You can also use this technique to make big letters smaller.

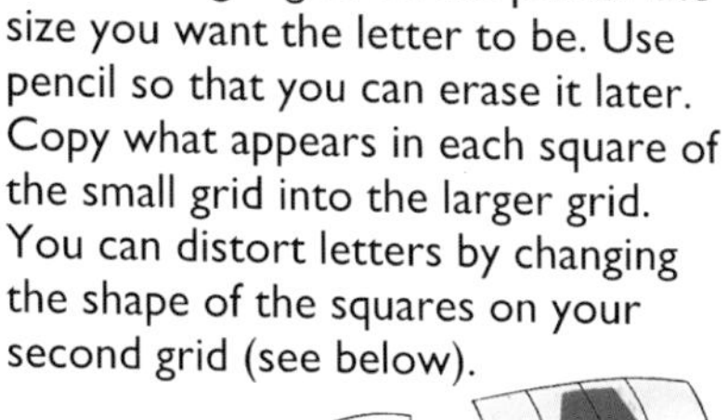

Draw a grid on tracing paper. Use about four squares to the height of the letter. Place the grid over the letter you want to copy, as above.

Draw a larger grid on the poster the size you want the letter to be. Use pencil so that you can erase it later. Copy what appears in each square of the small grid into the larger grid. You can distort letters by changing the shape of the squares on your second grid (see below).

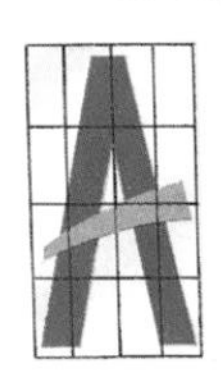

You can make the squares taller than they are wide...

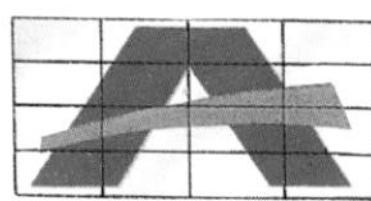

...or wider than they are tall...

...or you could draw a wavy grid...

...or a curved one.

Handwriting styles

Everyone's handwriting is different and it is as individual as your voice. Some people do handwriting as an art. This is called calligraphy.

Italic writing was devised about 500 years ago. It slopes gracefully to the right.

Calligraphy is based on traditional handwriting styles. Two calligraphy styles, called roman and italic, are shown on the right.

Roman calligraphy has developed over 2000 years. It is upright, with rounded letters.

Forming italic letters

Most italic letters are made up of several separate strokes. Take your pen off the paper between each stroke. Below are some letters to try. You can find out about italic pens on page 27 and there is an italic alphabet to copy on page 31.

This is an italic pen. Hold it so that the nib is at 45° to horizontal.

Width of stroke depends on the way your pen moves.

Form rounded shapes in two separate strokes.

Small finishing strokes are called serifs.

Do pen strokes in the directions shown.

Making letters larger

You can draw large, italic letter outlines using a twin-pointed pencil. To make one, tape two pencils together tightly.

The pencil points act like a nib.

You can buy twin-pointed felt-tips specially designed to make letters like this (see page 26).

Another calligraphy style

Copperplate is a style that was originally used for carving into glass or metal. You can copy copperplate styles using a thin nib. Do continuous, sweeping strokes keeping the pen on the paper. Next, go back and slightly thicken your downstrokes.

An example of copperplate engraving.

Letters flow into each other.

Your handwriting

Some people believe that you can tell what a person is like from their handwriting. This is called graphology.

Here are some signatures with different characteristics. You can develop your own signature and play with it like a design until you achieve a style you like.

Romantic

Aggressive

Decisive

Stenciling

You can create perfect lettering quickly and easily by using a set of letter stencils. Stencils are sheets of plastic or cardboard with shapes cut out. You draw around or paint inside the shapes. You can buy ready-made letter stencils. These come in various sizes.

Stencil brush

Stenciling with a brush

With a set of large letter stencils, you can create various textures using a stencil brush. Stencil brushes are thick with stiff bristles. You can buy them in art shops.

Mix some fairly thick paint and dip the end of the brush into it. Wipe the brush on spare paper until it is almost dry. Hold the stencil firmly and dab the bristles lightly over the letter. The more you go over the stencil the smoother the texture becomes.

Hold the brush upright and stencil right to the edge.

You could overlap the letters.

Too much paint causes splats.

Other stenciling ideas

These stenciling ideas are fairly messy so you will need to cover up everything except the letter you want.

Splattering with a paintbrush gives a random effect with different-shaped blobs.

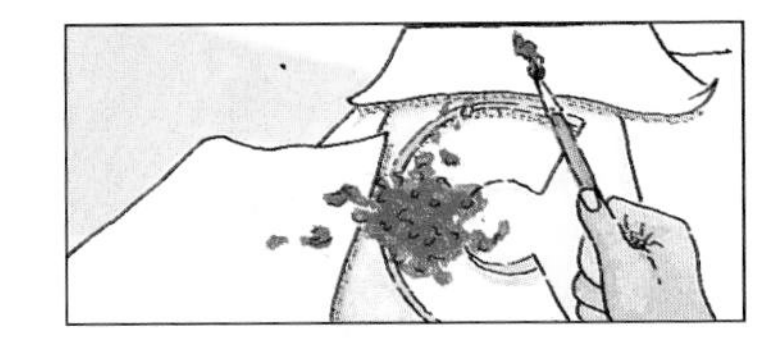

You can control the texture more easily by dabbing thick paint on with a sponge.

Flicking paint off the brush with a ruler and an old toothbrush gives fairly small dots of paint.

Illuminating letters

Before the age of printing, monks copied books by hand. They would often decorate the first letter of a page or a paragraph with beautiful shades and even gold leaf to make the letters shine. This is called illumination. You could do an illuminated letter at the beginning of a story or message.

Single letters

An illuminated letter can fill a whole page. You could make a card for someone by illuminating their initial. You could then shape a message around it.

Modern styles

It is fun to mix the old technique of illumination with a modern lettering style. You could begin a letter to a friend with a big greeting.

Magazine style

Magazines often use a large initial letter to make a page look more interesting.

Boxed letters

Draw a box outline in pencil. Then sketch the letter outline inside it.

Decorate the letter with different patterns, using felt-tips or paints.

You could draw a little scene around your boxed letter.

Tips

- Try to make sure the letter is not impossible to read.
- The style of the rest of the writing should match the illuminated letter. Try gothic or italic style if you want an ancient feel. There are gothic and italic alphabets to copy on pages 30-31.

What to use

- A hard pencil is best for sketching (see page 26).
- Use bright pencils, felt-tips or paint for your final decoration.
- You can buy gold and silver paint and pens from art shops. Metallic paint eventually loses its shine, though.

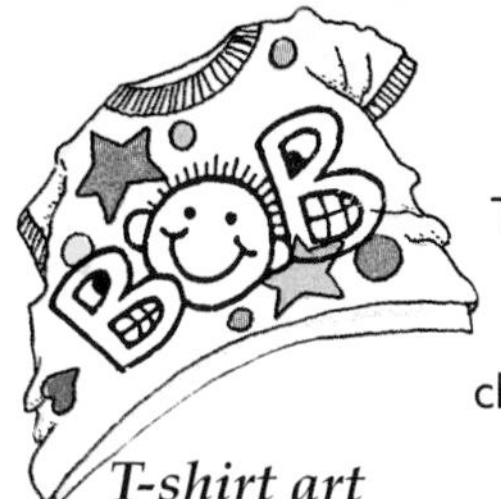

Lettering on fabric

To write on T-shirts, banners and flags, you can use fabric paint. Some fabric paints can only be used on natural materials such as cotton, so check the instructions before you do any lettering.

T-shirt art

Before you start lettering your T-shirt, draw the design on paper.

Pin the T-shirt flat on a stiff board and copy the design in pale chalk.

Now paint in the design. The chalk marks will wear off or wash out.

Bold, black letters on white T-shirts look very striking. This style is often used for protest messages.

Practical tips

- For crisp letter outlines, wear down the chalk to give it a sharp edge.
- Put paper (but not newspaper) between layers of fabric to stop paint seeping through.

Printing blocks

You can print on fabric using a printing block. Make a block by gluing a letter onto a piece of wood. The wood must be flat and the letter needs to be made from raised material, such as string or corrugated cardboard. Make the letters back to front so that they come out the right way when printed. Test that the letters are right by holding them up to a mirror.

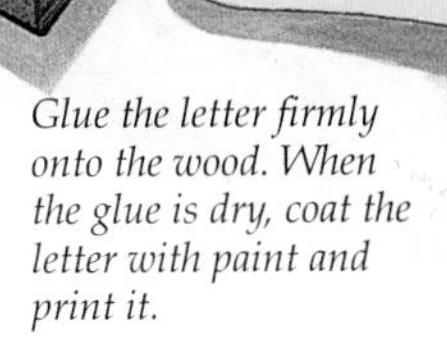

Glue the letter firmly onto the wood. When the glue is dry, coat the letter with paint and print it.

Flags and banners

It is hard to read letters on flags so use short words. You could fly a flag outside on your birthday with your age on it. For longer messages, you could try doing lots of single letters across a long stretch of bunting, like the one below.

Try drawing a banner in miniature first. This makes it easier to work out the design. For example, if your banner is to be 3m (10ft) long, scale it down to 30cm (1ft). Use the grid technique (see page 13) to copy the design.

Dramatic lettering

Here are some techniques that can make lettering look very dramatic. They work particularly well with big capital letters. You could use thesetechniques on banners or posters.

Letters in perspective

Using a fairly hard pencil, such as a 2H (see page 26), mark three dots on a vertical line. Then draw a line farther up the page to represent the horizon.

Horizon

Space dots out evenly on a vertical line.

Mark a point on the horizon. This is called the vanishing point. Join each dot to it. Use these lines as guidelines for your lettering.

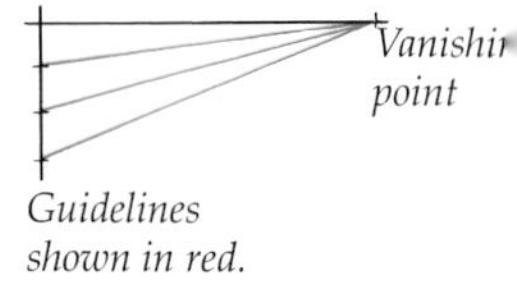

Guidelines shown in red.

Do the letters closer together near the vanishing point. Drawings which show distance and depth accurately are "in perspective".

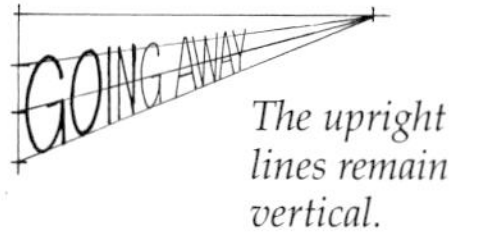

The upright lines remain vertical.

Shadow lettering

Draw the letter outline, a horizon and a vanishing point. Add a line where the top of the shadow will go.

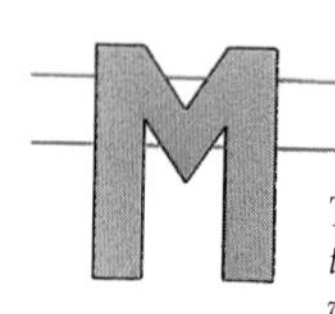

Horizon

The top of the shadow will fall on this line.

Draw lines from the uprights to the vanishing point. These show where to put the shadows of the uprights.

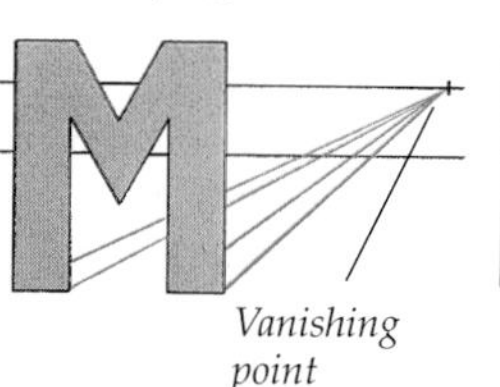

Vanishing point

Use your judgement to position the other lines of the shadow. Experiment with them until they look right.

Rub out the guidelines.

Word tower

This word tower is decorated to look like a worn stone monument. Here is how to draw one like it.

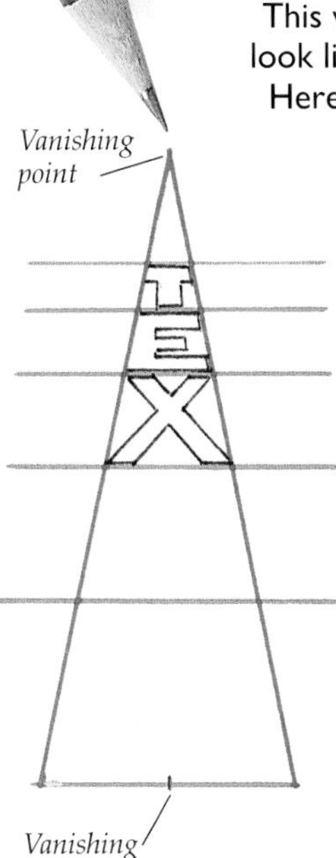

1. Draw a base line showing the width of the lowest letter. Mark a vanishing point in the middle of it. Mark another vanishing point high up, directly above it.

2. Draw guidelines from either end of this base line to the top vanishing point.

3. Draw guidelines to show the height of each letter. Letters get shorter as they get higher up. Then draw in the fronts of the letters.

4. To make the letters look solid, first draw lines from the corners and edges to the lower vanishing point.

Construction lines from letter corners and edges.

5. Shade in the undersides of the letters. One at a time, ink in a chipped outline and erase the construction lines. Finally, do a rough surface.

Comic strip lettering

A comic strip story is told in pictures and words. The lettering has several jobs to do. It shows what people say or think, adds to the sense of drama and provides sound effects.

Round frame

No frame

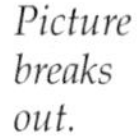

Picture frames

Varying the style of the boxes around the pictures, called frames, keeps the strip lively. Draw frames freehand to give your strip a relaxed look.

Square frame

Picture breaks out.

Oblong frame

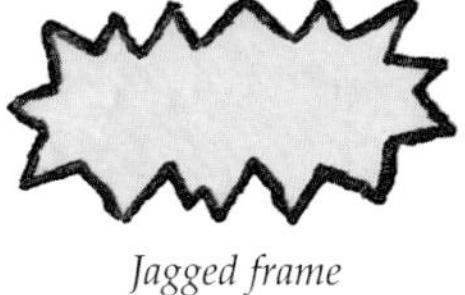

Jagged frame

Sound effects

A sound effect is a sort of picture of a sound. This short strip shows how they can be used.

Here are some more examples of sound effect styles.

Dust clouds represent an explosion.

Jagged bubble shows a sharp sound.

Wobbly letters suggest a squelch.

Speech bubbles

A speech bubble can show how words are said. For instance, small letters in a big bubble make words look quiet. People read from left to right and top to bottom, so position speech bubbles in a frame so that they will be read in the right order.

Positioning letters

Speech bubbles can look neat if you position the letters with care. First, count the letters and spaces in each line. Count fat letters like w and m as three units. Medium letters such as h, n and o are two units. Spaces and thin letters such as i and t are one unit. A capital letter has one extra unit.

Draw a vertical line. Put an equal number of units either side of it.

Use a thin black pen for the letters. Then draw a bubble outline around them.

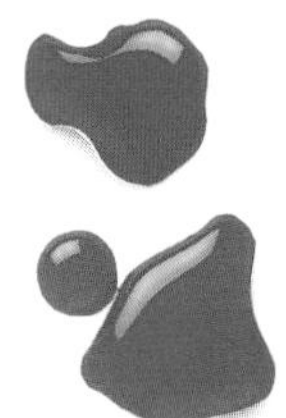

Lettering kit

Here is a guide to some of the materials which you can use for lettering. All of these are available at art materials shops and you can buy some of them at an ordinary stationers.

Pencils

Pencils are marked from 9H to 7B depending on how hard (H) or soft (B for black) they are. Use a medium hard (2H) pencil for sketching letters.

A medium hard (2H) pencil will mark paper easily, but will not smudge.

Technical drawing pens

A technical drawing pen with a fine point gives even-looking letters and thin, precise outlines. These pens are also good for comic strip lettering.

Technical drawing pens are expensive but give tidy results.

Felt-tips

Felt-tips can have different shapes and sizes of tips, for different uses. For example a fine felt-tip is a cheaper alternative to a technical drawing pen.

A fine felt-tip is good for small letters.

Felt-tip shaped for italic letters.

This pen gives parallel lines which you can fill in with a different shade.

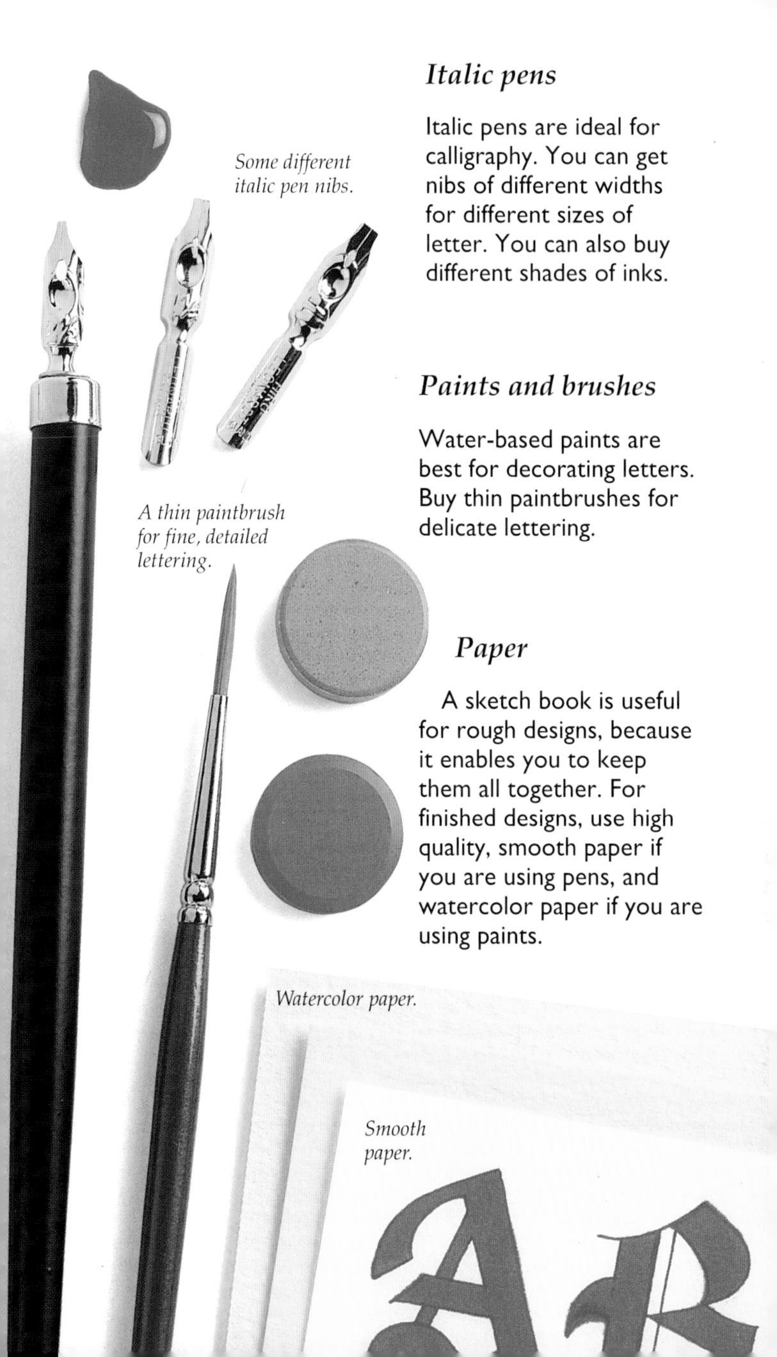

Italic pens

Italic pens are ideal for calligraphy. You can get nibs of different widths for different sizes of letter. You can also buy different shades of inks.

Some different italic pen nibs.

Paints and brushes

Water-based paints are best for decorating letters. Buy thin paintbrushes for delicate lettering.

A thin paintbrush for fine, detailed lettering.

Paper

A sketch book is useful for rough designs, because it enables you to keep them all together. For finished designs, use high quality, smooth paper if you are using pens, and watercolor paper if you are using paints.

Watercolor paper.

Smooth paper.

Alphabets to copy

Here are some alphabets for you to trace or copy. The alphabet below is a serif alphabet. It has finishing strokes, known as serifs.

Serif alphabet

ABCDEFGHIJKLM

NOPQRSTUVWXYZ

abcdefghijklmnopqrstuvwxyz

1234567890

Sans-serif alphabet

This is a sans-serif alphabet. It has no finishing strokes. *Sans* means "without" in French.

ABCDEFGHIJKLM
NOPQRSTUVWXYZ
abcdefghijklmnopqrstuvwxyz
1234567890

Gothic alphabet

Gothic alphabets, like this, use heavy script letters that were used in the 15th-18th centuries. They are also known as "black letter".

ABCDEFGHIJKLM

NOPQRSTUVWXYZ

abcdefghijklmnopqrstuvwxyz

1234567890

Italic alphabet

This is an italic alphabet. Italic alphabets slant slightly to the right. It has small finishing strokes, so it is also a serif alphabet.

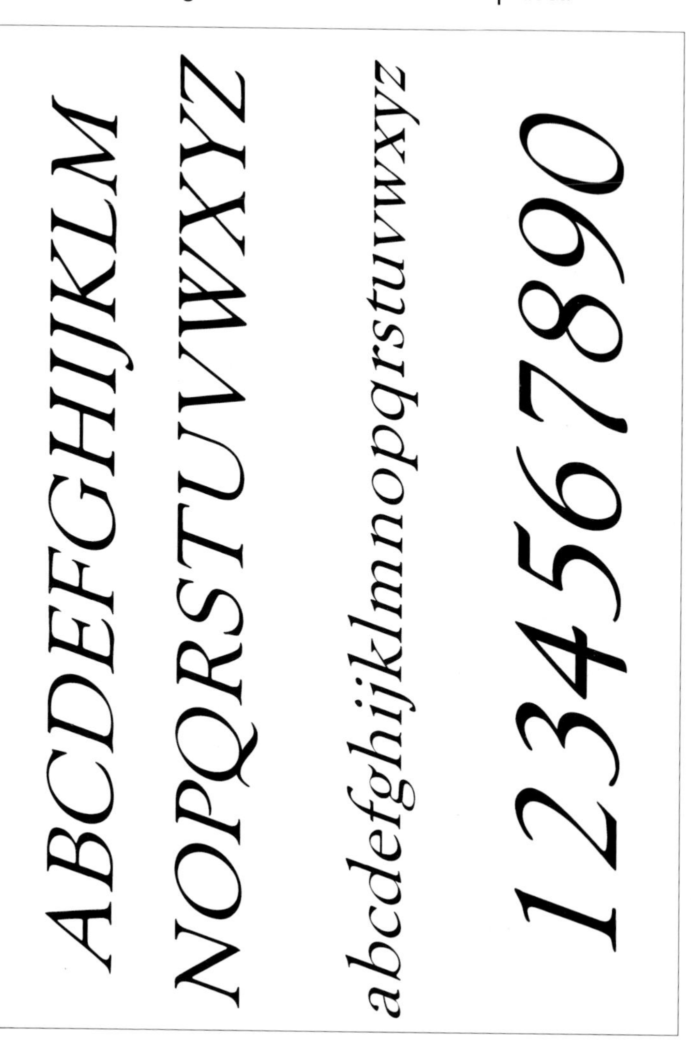

Index

This book is based on material previously published in *How to Draw Lettering.*

First published in 1995 by Usborne Publishing Ltd, Usborne House, 83-85 Saffron Hill, London EC1N 8RT, England.

First published in America August 1995. AE

Printed in Italy.